Laugh-a-Long Readers™

by Diane Namm
illustrated by Wayne Becker

New York / London
www.sterlingpublishing.com/kids

Library of Congress Cataloging-in-Publication Data

Namm, Diane.
Laugh out loud jokes / by Diane Namm, illustrated by Wayne Becker.
p. cm. -- (Laugh-a-long readers)
Originally published: New York : Barnes & Noble Books, 2004.
ISBN-13: 978-1-4027-5002-1
ISBN-10: 1-4027-5002-1
1. Wit and humor, Juvenile. I. Becker, Wayne. II. Title.
PN6166.N36 2008
818'.5402--dc22
2007030249

2 4 6 8 10 9 7 5 3 1

Published 2008 by Sterling Publishing Co., Inc.
387 Park Avenue South, New York, NY 10016
Originally published and © 2004 by Barnes and Noble, Inc.,
under the title *Laugh-a-Long Readers: Silly Jokes*
Distributed in Canada by Sterling Publishing
c/o Canadian Manda Group, 165 Dufferin Street
Toronto, Ontario, Canada M6K 3H6
Distributed in the United Kingdom by GMC Distribution Services
Castle Place, 166 High Street, Lewes, East Sussex, England BN7 1XU
Distributed in Australia by Capricorn Link (Australia) Pty. Ltd.
P.O. Box 704, Windsor, NSW 2756, Australia

Written by Diane Namm
Illustrated by Wayne Becker
Designed by Jo Obarowski

Printed in China

Sterling ISBN-13: 978-1-4027-5002-1
ISBN-10: 1-4027-5002-1

For information about custom editions, special sales, premium and corporate purchases, please contact Sterling Special Sales Department at 800-805-5489 or specialsales@sterlingpublishing.com.

What has four wheels and roars down the road?

A lion on a skateboard.

How do you fix a gorilla robot?

Use a monkey wrench.

What has four wheels and flies?

A garbage truck.

Why don't bananas get lonely?

They go around in bunches.

What is it called when a queen has a sore throat?

A royal pain in the neck.

How does a baker get rich?

He makes a lot of dough.

What do you do when an 800-pound gorilla asks you to dance?

Run.

Why did the mother bunny take her baby to the doctor?

He was feeling a little jumpy.

How do you stop a fish from smelling?

Put a clothespin on its nose.

Where does an otter put its money?

In a riverbank.

What is harder to catch the faster you run?

Your breath.

What room has no window, no door, and no walls?

A mushroom.

Why did the orange lose the race?

It ran out of juice.

Why does the ocean roar?

It has crabs in its bed.